Acting Edition

One of the Good Ones

by Gloria Calderón Kellett

||SAMUEL FRENCH||

FOR PRODUCTION INQUIRIES

UNITED STATES AND CANADA
info@concordtheatricals.com
1-866-979-0447

UNITED KINGDOM AND EUROPE
licensing@concordtheatricals.co.uk
020-7054-7298

Each title is subject to availability from Concord Theatricals Corp., depending upon country of performance. Please be aware that *ONE OF THE GOOD ONES* may not be licensed by Concord Theatricals Corp. in your territory. Professional and amateur producers should contact the nearest Concord Theatricals Corp. office or licensing partner to verify availability.

No one shall make any changes in this title(s) for the purpose of production. No part of this book may be reproduced, stored in a retrieval system, scanned, uploaded, or transmitted in any form, by any means, now known or yet to be invented, including mechanical, electronic, digital, photocopying, recording, videotaping, or otherwise, without the prior written permission of the publisher. No one shall share this title(s), or any part of this title(s), through any social media or file hosting websites.

For all inquiries regarding motion picture, television, online/digital and other media rights, please contact Concord Theatricals Corp.

MUSIC AND THIRD-PARTY MATERIALS USE NOTE

Licensees are solely responsible for obtaining formal written permission from copyright owners to use copyrighted music and/or other copyrighted third-party materials (e.g. artworks, logos) in the performance of this play and are strongly cautioned to do so. If no such permission is obtained by the licensee, then the licensee must use only original music and materials that the licensee owns and controls. Licensees are solely responsible and liable for clearances of all third-party copyrighted materials, including without limitation music, and shall indemnify the copyright owners of the play(s) and their licensing agent, Concord Theatricals Corp., against any costs, expenses, losses and liabilities arising from the use of such copyrighted third-party materials by licensees. For music, please contact the appropriate music licensing authority in your territory for the rights to any incidental music.

IMPORTANT BILLING AND CREDIT REQUIREMENTS

If you have obtained performance rights to this title, please refer to your licensing agreement for important billing and credit requirements.

ONE OF THE GOOD ONES was first produced by Pasadena Playhouse (Danny Feldman, Producing Artistic Director) in Los Angeles, California, and premiered there on March 17, 2024. The production was directed by Kimberly Senior, with scenic design by Tanya Orellana, costume design by Denitsa Bliznakova, lighting design by Jaymi Lee Smith, and sound design by Jeff Gardner and Andrea Allmond. The production stage manager was David S. Franklin. The cast was as follows:

ILANA . . . . Lana Parrilla

PEDRO. . . . . .Santino Jimenez

YOLI. . . . . .Isabella Gomez

ENRIQUE. . . . . Carlos Gomez

MARCOS . . . . .Nico Greetham

ONE OF THE GOOD ONES was subsequently produced by the Old Globe Theater (Barry Edelstein, Erna Finci Viterbi Artistic Director; Timothy J. Shields, Audrey S. Geisel Managing Director) in San Diego, California, opening on May 24th, 2025. The production was directed by Kimberly Senior, with scenic design by Takeshi Kata, costume design by Sarita Fellows, lighting design by Jaymi Lee Smith, and sound design by Jeff Gardner and Andrea Allmond. Casting was by Joe Gery with Caparelliotis Casting. The production stage manager was Chandra R.M. Anthenill, the assistant stage manager was Karla Garcia, and the stage management swing was Amanda Salmons. The cast was as follows:

ILANA . . . . Angelique Cabral

PEDRO. . . . . .Santino Jimenez

YOLI. . . . . Cree

ENRIQUE. . . . . Benito Martinez

MARCOS . . . . .Nico Greetham

CHARACTERS

ILANA – Late 40s+, Mexican American and Puerto Rican, a successful businesswoman.

PEDRO – 20s–40s, Latino man.

YOLI – 22, Latina, recent college graduate, Ilana and Enrique's daughter.

ENRIQUE – Late 40s+, Latino, a successful businessman.

MARCOS – 24, White, Yoli's boyfriend.

SETTING

Enrique and Ilana's living room and dining room in a beautiful, upscale home in Pasadena, California.

TIME

Summer of 2024.

AUTHOR'S NOTES

Note On Character Identity

Disclaimer: Ilana is written as Mexican and Puerto Rican to serve the story, with a focus on her Mexican heritage. However, we encourage producers to adapt the character's background to align with the authentic heritage of the actress cast in the role. For example, if the actress is Dominican, Ilana can be portrayed as Mexican and Dominican. Identity is complex – and that complexity is at the heart of this play. Our hope is to reflect that nuance by honoring the lived experience of the performer. Thank you for helping us tell this story with both integrity and care.

Note On Production

As the audience leaves the theater, they should be offered candy.

(An old fashioned Spanish love song like "Quizás, Quizás, Quizás" by Trio Los Panchos plays.[*] As the song ends the lights begin to fade to black.)

(Lights up on an opulent, open plan home. On the right is the living room and on the left is the dining room – there is a pass-through to the left of the dining room that goes into a kitchen but not much can be seen through the pass-through of the kitchen itself. The decor is modern but expensive with a hint of Latino influence but nothing over the top. There is original art, there are sculptures. Money lives here.)

(The doorbell rings. Nothing.)

(It rings again.)

ILANA. *(Offstage.)* Coming!

(A woman, **ILANA GOMEZ**, *Latina, rushes to the table, which is beautifully set, and places a pitcher of water on it. She then runs across the stage to the door on the far right. She*

---

[*] A license to produce *One of the Good Ones* does not include a performance license for "Quizás, Quizás, Quizás." The publisher and author suggest that the licensee contact ASCAP or BMI to ascertain the music publisher and contact such music publisher to license or acquire permission for performance of the song. If a license or permission is unattainable for "Quizás, Quizás, Quizás," the licensee may not use the song in *One of the Good Ones* but should create an original composition in a similar style or use a similar song in the public domain. For further information, please see the Music and Third-Party Materials Use Note on page iii.

*checks her makeup in a mirror to the right of the door before opening it. There stands a Latino man, **PEDRO**, holding a large floral arrangement.)*

ILANA. The flowers! Perfect timing. These are beautiful! My daughter is introducing us to a boy for the first time tonight. Ah!

> *(**PEDRO** just stares at **ILANA**. **ILANA** puts two and two together.)*

Oh, lo siento. Uh – No hablo Español.

PEDRO. *No hay problema.*

> *(Panic starts to set in.)*

ILANA. Uh... *Me llamo Ilana.*

PEDRO. *Me llamo Pedro.*

ILANA. Pedro! Great. Wait. Uh...*un*...uh, minute-o?

> *(Wait, she got it right!)*

Minuto! Sometimes it's right there.

> *(Nothing from **PEDRO**.)*

(Yelling off.) YOLI!

> *(Then.)*

Mi, uh, daughter *hable Español. Yo tengo que* – learn. *Soy Latina.* I know I look like a white girl.

PEDRO. Uh ha.

ILANA. Heard it my whole life. But *soy* Mexican *y* Puerto Rican. Me. *Yo.* We didn't cross the border, the border crossed us!

> *(She laughs. He isn't amused.)*

PEDRO. *(Couldn't care less.)* Okay.

ILANA. But my parents *Mi padres* they told me to learn English. Because that is what they were told. This is America speak English! *Ingles!! No Español.*

(Realizing.) Not you. <u>I'm</u> not saying that – <u>they</u> said that. *Gente,* amiright? So... YOLI!

(Suddenly a woman, **YOLI**, *22, Latina, enters.)*

YOLI. Yeah?

ILANA. Oh, thank God. He doesn't speak English. Can you –

YOLI. Speak Spanish? Sure.

(To the **MAN**.*) Hola. ¿Cómo puedo ayudarte?*

PEDRO. *¿Dónde quieres las flores?*

YOLI. He just wants to know where to put the flowers down.

ILANA. *(To* **YOLI**.*)* Of course!

(Motions for the table and yells.)

There! On the table there!

YOLI. You're yelling. He can hear you.

(To **PEDRO**.*) En la mesa allí, por favor.*

(He begins to bring the flowers to the table.)

How's that Duolingo going?

ILANA. Obviously, *no bueno.* See, this is why I forced you to learn!

*(***ILANA** *grabs cash from her nearby purse and gives* **PEDRO** *a wad of it.)*

PEDRO. *Ella ya pagó.*

YOLI. He says you already paid.

ILANA. Tell him it's my guilt and to take it, *por favor.*

YOLI. *Tómalo. Es tu propina.*

PEDRO. *Gracias.*

    (**PEDRO** *pulls a phone out of his pocket and hands it to* **ILANA**.)

Firma aquí con su dedo, por favor.

YOLI. He wants you to sign it. With your finger.

ILANA. Oh, fancy. Digital. You go, Pedro.

    (*She hands him back his phone.*)

Uh, wait, wait. *Agua? Agua!*

    (**ILANA** *grabs the pitcher and pours him a glass of water.*)

PEDRO. *Eso no es necesario. Estoy bien.*

YOLI. *Es mas fácil si la dejas.*

ILANA. Drink. Hot outside! *Bebé!*

YOLI. *Bebé* means baby.

ILANA. What's "drink"?

YOLI. *Beber.*

ILANA. That's what I said.

YOLI. No, you said *Bebé.* Very different.

ILANA. Is it? See, this is why it's so hard for me to learn!

YOLI. *Se siente mal y quiere que bebas el agua. No tienes que hacerlo. Ella está un poquita loca.*

    (**ILANA** *knows the word "loca" and gives* **YOLI** *a look.* **PEDRO** *obliges.*)

PEDRO. Okay.

(He puts the cash in his pocket and the phone on the side table and takes the glass. He drinks half of it.)

Mmmmmm.

*(**ILANA** looks encouragingly. She is desperate for his approval. He knows this so he finishes it. She is pleased and gives him a thumbs up.)*

Gracias.

ILANA. No, <u>you</u> *gracias.*

*(**PEDRO** looks at her confused and nods as he begins to exit. Leaving the phone. No one notices.)*

PEDRO. *Que tengan un buen día.*

*(When the door closes **ILANA** exhales.)*

ILANA. God that was stressful.

YOLI. Okay Mom.

*(**YOLI** laughs.)*

ILANA. I heard you say *loca.* I understand what *loca* means! 'Cause of Ricky Martin.

YOLI. Who's Ricky Martin?

*(**ILANA** just shoots her a death look.)*

I'm kidding. I just like making you feel old sometimes.

ILANA. Mean! You're different since graduating from college.

YOLI. I know my social security number by heart now. Maybe it's that.

ILANA. No...something is different. Like...you carry yourself differently.

YOLI. You didn't expect to pay all of that money just for me to come out the same.

(**ENRIQUE**, *50s, is revealed.*)

ENRIQUE. She's right, you are different.

ILANA. Wait, have you been listening this whole time?

ENRIQUE. *(To* **ILANA**.*)* What whole time?

ILANA. Since the doorbell? Since the flowers?

ENRIQUE. *(To* **ILANA**.*)* Yes.

ILANA. *(Still on* **ENRIQUE**.*)* Why didn't you help me?

ENRIQUE. You're always saying you want to practice your Spanish.

ILANA. I'm sweating here.

ENRIQUE. *Pobrecita. Ella está nerviosa porque va a conocer a tu amigo.*

YOLI. *¿Pero papi, por qué estás hablando en Español? Tú sabes que a ella no le gusta.*

ILANA. Oh, and now Spanish?

YOLI. Sorry, Mom. He's sucking me in.

(*Then.*)

Papi, ya.

ENRIQUE. *Creo que debemos hablar un poquito más.*

YOLI. *Y tú dices que soy yo la que causa problemas. Tú eres peor!*

ENRIQUE. *Ay, Yoli. Solo me estoy divirtiendo. Tú eres la que ha estado un poco seria desde que llegaste.*

ILANA. Enrique, I'm going to scream or cry or both if you two don't stop. I'm going through menopause. I'm hot. I'm cold. I'm horny. Mercy. Please.

ENRIQUE. When are you horny? Why am I missing out on that?

YOLI. Can you please talk about this when I'm not in the room?

ENRIQUE. Yes, 'cause parents being attracted to each other is so gross.

YOLI. It's not gross. I just don't need to hear about it.

(*Then.*)

Maybe it's a little gross.

ENRIQUE. I thought you wanted us all to communicate more?

YOLI. Yes, but –

ENRIQUE. No. No but. Do you want to communicate more or not? 'Cause you can't pick and choose.

YOLI. Sure you can. Mom does it all the time.

ILANA. What do I do?

YOLI. You only want to talk about happy things.

ILANA. What's wrong with that?

YOLI. Uh, things aren't always happy. Sometimes you need to talk about things that are unpleasant.

ILANA. But can't we choose to focus on the happy things?

YOLI. I mean if you want to go through the world going (*Puts fingers in ears.*) LALALA. Then, I guess you can, but I would prefer not to.

ILANA. I don't do that.

YOLI. *Mami,* you have literally said you don't watch the news 'cause it's too sad.

ILANA. Have you seen local news?

YOLI. You're only proving my point.

ILANA. What point?

YOLI. That we need to be free to talk about things! Good and bad things.

ENRIQUE. Well, now you're actually just proving my point. 'Cause if you want to be able to talk about bad things then you also have to hear about me being horny for your mom.

YOLI. You know, it might just be the word "horny." It's so ew.

ENRIQUE. Ew?

YOLI. Come on, you have words that gross you out. Like ointment.

ENRIQUE. Ew.

ILANA. This is a ridiculous conversation.

ENRIQUE. I'm not opposed to "hot for" –

(Pitching it to her.) I am hot for your mother. Does that trouble you less?

YOLI. I don't think we need to solve it right now.

ENRIQUE. You suddenly seem so desperate for us to treat you as an adult and then you keep behaving like a child. That's all.

YOLI. You say that like it's not a dig and it is such a dig.

ENRIQUE. It's not meant as a dig. It's meant as an observation. You want us to see you as an adult? Act like an adult.

YOLI. I am an adult. I've graduated from college.

(Stamping her foot.) With honors!

ENRIQUE. Yeah, that's not helping.

YOLI. Fair. I just have things – important things I want to talk to you about.

ILANA. Later. Can you help me finish setting up?

YOLI. But –   **ENRIQUE**. Yep!

(They walk over to the dining room and help.)

ILANA. I want the place to look perfect when we meet your new friend.

YOLI. Boyfriend.

ILANA. Yes. That's what I meant.

YOLI. Serious boyfriend.

ENRIQUE. Serious? That's new information.

YOLI. It's not. I've said serious before.

ILANA. Mmmm? "Promising"? Yes.

ENRIQUE. "Potential"? Yes.

ILANA. "Serious" is new.

YOLI. Well, it's serious.

ILANA. Huh.

ENRIQUE. The table looks beautiful, *mi amor.*

YOLI. It always does.

ILANA. I may not be able to cook but I can make things pretty.

> *(**ENRIQUE** opens the hutch to grab the glasses. He hands some to **YOLI** and they finish the table over the following.)*

YOLI. You really didn't need to do all of this. Especially the extra tip you paid Pedro 'cause you always get so weird around Latino workers.

ILANA. No, I don't. That's ridiculous.

YOLI. You just did it. Dad tell her.

ILANA. What? What did I do?

YOLI. "*Hola* my best friend, Pedro! I'm so comfortable with Latinos as subordinates that I have a deep need to make them my new bestie." Totally normal.

ENRIQUE. See. That. That is new. We were having a nice moment. And you had to find something negative and poke us with it.

YOLI. I just made an observation and now we're talking about it.

ENRIQUE. You used to just enjoy when we were all peacefully talking about something.

ILANA. I am not "weird" around Latino workers.

(Then.)

Am I weird around Latino workers?

YOLI. I'm just saying a man had flowers that you ordered and you had a full freak out because you felt such guilt at not being able to speak his language to him.

ILANA. It's not just that. It's way more complicated than that.

YOLI. What then?

ILANA. Let's please just talk about something else.

YOLI. No, Mom. We can't just put off conversations because they might be unpleasant.

ILANA. Of course we can. People have been doing it for millennia!

ENRIQUE. Did your last semester of college include a class called "how to push your parents' buttons post graduation"?

YOLI. You're so dramatic.

ENRIQUE. I'm so dramatic? Listen young lady –

ILANA. Don't fight. Fine. Fine. I'll talk about it. I guess, when I'm with Latino workers it makes me, like, hyper-aware of my behavior. 'Cause I remember all the stories my *abuela* told me about when she used to clean houses. And how awful it was for her and how badly people with money treated her – either like she wasn't human or they'd just ignore her completely – and I just don't want to be like that.

YOLI. So your weirdness comes from a place of actually wanting to make someone feel valued?

ILANA. Yes. Exactly.

YOLI. See, that's nice. Your weirdness comes from a good place.

ILANA. Can you stop saying "weirdness"? I'm doing my best out here...

YOLI. Mom, you're doing amazing! You own your own PR firm. You are, like, this incredible businesswoman who has not only built an empire, but also built generational wealth. You are your ancestors' wildest dreams.

ILANA. You're gonna make me cry.

YOLI. Oh, Mom.

ILANA. I just wish there wasn't such massive inequality – still. And that's where the Spanish thing stings. I got such mixed messages from my family growing up. They were so on me about not having an accent – "speak like the lady on the TV, Ilana!" So that's what I focused on. My abuela said they got hit with rulers in school for speaking Spanish. You were failed for having an accent! If they heard you even whispering Spanish they'd make you write it down and bury the paper in the ground. Imagine that. So I didn't learn because they were scared for me to learn. I wish I <u>could</u> speak it because, I don't know, it feels like it would tie me to my culture more. Like... I shouldn't have to speak it but

I want to speak it but I haven't taken the time to learn to speak it. But if I really cared then wouldn't I have made it a priority – 'Cause I certainly made sure my daughter could speak it so why didn't I ever do it and the shame spiral begins again!

YOLI. Oh wow. I didn't know.

ILANA. Ugh, why are we talking about this right now? This is not the time.

YOLI. That all sounds impossible to navigate. And we can't blame my abuelos because they probably had a tough time because of their accents, and they wanted things to be easier for you. It's a lot. And it shouldn't be all yours to carry. Release the shame! And, I'll practice Spanish with you. How about that?

(**YOLI** *hugs her* **MOM**.)

ILANA. *(Softening.)* Gosh, that's nice. I'd love that.

(To **ENRIQUE**.*)* We raised such a nice person.

ENRIQUE. Sometimes.

(Beat.)

YOLI. *Bueno, mami. Qué mas nececitas para la mesa?*

ILANA. Oh, you're starting right now… That's so nice but not right now. Spanish later. After serious boyfriend.

YOLI. Okay. The table looks amazing.

ILANA. Thank you.

(**YOLI** *pulls out her phone.)*

YOLI. Post worthy.

ENRIQUE. Wait.

(He pulls out his phone to add more light.)

YOLI. Better. Thanks, papi.

ENRIQUE. You're welcome. See, I support your hobby.

YOLI. Job. It's my job.

ENRIQUE. It's not.

YOLI. Just when I feel like we're having a breakthrough –

ILANA. Guys. No fighting. Let's not start this again.

YOLI. That is your intergenerational trauma talking and I am trying to liberate you two from the suffocating blanket of morality that your ancestors placed on you!

ILANA. Can liberation come tomorrow?

ENRIQUE. You want to talk about all of this uncomfortable stuff, but if we want to talk about something you don't like, it's shut down. That's all I'm saying.

YOLI. Thank you for saying that. I'm gonna try to be more aware and hear you out because what I want is to have productive and meaningful dialogue.

   (Then.)

See. I didn't have a meltdown because you called me out on something.

ENRIQUE. And then you rub our face in the fact that we're not as "evolved" as you are. That's your other move.

ILANA. Guys.

YOLI. I have no moves. This isn't a game. I just wanna talk to you guys.

ILANA. Later. Later.

(Then, to **YOLI.***)* I love this dress you picked out.

YOLI. I knew you'd like it.

ILANA. And I'm obviously gonna change from this chancla to a heel before he arrives. Don't worry.

YOLI. I wasn't worried.

ILANA. Do you want to do a darker lip?

YOLI. No, I'm good.

ILANA. You sure because I think –

YOLI. Mom. I'm good.

ILANA. Okay. Okay. It would look better but okay.

> *(Okay, she's laid the groundwork...* **YOLI** *is ready.)*

YOLI. I am so excited for you guys to finally meet Marcos.

ILANA. So are we. We're just excited that you're finally bringing someone home. He must special. I mean, who knows... Maybe he's the one? Oh my god, I need a shot.

(To **ENRIQUE**.*)* Baby, aren't you even a little nervous?

ENRIQUE. Nah. This is gonna be fun. He's gonna be so scared of me. And I'm going to really enjoy that.

YOLI. Gross, Dad. That is the most patriarchal B.S. I've heard in awhile.

ENRIQUE. I feel like you just learned the word "patriarchy" and are excited to use it a lot.

YOLI. See, this is where <u>you</u> are infuriating. Do you not think that patriarchy is real? Because you're being casual and it's not cute, Dad.

ENRIQUE. First of all, I'm always cute. Second of all, yes, I get that men run the world. I am not denying that. But you are the most wonderful young woman I know. So, I gotta suss out the person that thinks they are good enough to spend time with you. He's got to be deserving of you. And I need to know that he knows that you are spectacular. Because you are my little girl, and you are a prize to be treasured!

YOLI. It was going so well until you turned me into a prize.

ENRIQUE. You know what I mean. That was all so nice what I said.

ILANA. It was. It was.

YOLI. Up until the part where I became a trophy... Sure?

ENRIQUE. Ay, Yoli. You just like to focus on the bad.

YOLI. You don't understand how you sound!

ENRIQUE. It's exhausting. You are exhausting.

YOLI. *(Mocking.)* Bad trophy! You should just be pretty and not talk.

ENRIQUE. That is not what I mean!

ILANA. Stop it. Please. I'd like to hear more about this young man before we meet him. Focus, people.

YOLI. Okay.

ENRIQUE. Fine.

ILANA. Good. So tell us stuff... So his name is Marcos.

YOLI. Yes. Marcos Cruise. He's really hot like stupid hot – not that that is important but it's a fact. And he's also very smart. Born in Mexico but his family came to the U.S. when he was seven. His dad works for the Dodgers.

ENRIQUE. The Doyers. I love that!

YOLI. Right? And his mom is a Spanish teacher.

ENRIQUE. Maybe she can help teach your mom.

ILANA. Easy.

ENRIQUE. Well, we are looking forward to meeting him.

YOLI. Good. Great. Because it is very serious.

ILANA. Did it just go from serious to very serious?

ENRIQUE. I caught that, too.

YOLI. I just have a lot to fill you in on.

ENRIQUE. Okay. Fill us in.

YOLI. Okay. Yeah. I'm an adult person. So, I'm just gonna say it, I am an adult and I'm gonna say it. I lost my virginity to Marcos. We're having sex. It is very good.

ENRIQUE. What. No. No. No. No. No.

ILANA. *(So moved.)* Oh baby. I am so thankful that you felt comfortable enough to share that with us.

ENRIQUE. No we're not.

ILANA. I am.

ENRIQUE. Why did you tell us that? I didn't want to know that.

ILANA. I did.

YOLI. I'm not ashamed about it. I am a grown woman and I'd like to be treated as such.

ENRIQUE. Are your bills on autopay?

YOLI. What? No. What does that have to do with –

ENRIQUE. Then you aren't an adult. Having sex does not make you an adult.

ILANA. Enrique, I was eighteen, when we first –

ENRIQUE. You were a way more mature eighteen-year-old.

YOLI. Seriously?

ENRIQUE. We were married. <u>And</u> I had three jobs.

YOLI. So having more than one job gives you a license to bone? Cool.

ILANA. Yoli.

ENRIQUE. No, but you don't even have one!

YOLI. I do have a job. I'm an influencer!

ENRIQUE. That isn't a job! *Chica!*

YOLI. Yes. It. Is!

(*Then.*)

And what does having a job have to do with –

ILANA. Honey, we're so happy for you.

ENRIQUE. No, we're not!

ILANA. Yes, we are. Because we aren't our parents and we want our daughter to talk to us.

(*This shuts* **ENRIQUE** *up.*)

(*Then, earnest, to* **YOLI**.) Did you bleed? 'Cause I bled. But they say girls these days don't bleed 'cause they used tampons which breaks the hymen. My mom had me so freaked out about toxic shock syndrome that I always used those huge pads – I had like a freaking pillow between my legs and turns out no one I know ever got toxic shock syndrome, so maybe it was one of those fake things Latina moms tell their daughters like going outside with wet hair will kill you. Anyway, lalala. Since you got home you've seemed so different and so, I don't know, mysterious and honestly I'm relieved 'cause I knew there was something...and now I know what it is. And I'm just so happy you're confiding in us and my hope is that it was a beautiful experience for you.

ENRIQUE. Ew.

ILANA. Ew? Really? Who's the immature one now?

(*To* **YOLI**.) Ignore him.

(*To* **ENRIQUE**.) This is one of the biggest moments of my daughter's life. Getting her period, bra shopping, losing her virginity, planning her wedding. These things are huge for a mom. A mother dreams of moments like these, Enrique!

ENRIQUE. A father has nightmares about moments like these, Ilana.

ILANA. Well things can't always be about you and your comfort.

ENRIQUE. Are you really starting with me right now?

ILANA. I'd argue you're starting with me!

ENRIQUE. How am I starting with you?

ILANA. Uh, your tone for one.

ENRIQUE. I don't want to hear about my daughter having sex. There is nothing wrong with that.

> *(Then...the doorbell rings. A beat. Silence.)*

Well, shit.

> *(He goes to open the door when –)*

ILANA. Wait! Karate chop the pillows!

YOLI. What?

ILANA. Karate chop the pillows! You know the drill.

> *(She demonstrates her way of refreshing the pillows. They quickly go around chopping the pillows in a hurry.)*

(To **YOLI**.*)* And please don't give me a lecture about how saying karate chop is somehow problematic because I will combust and then you'll need to explain to your serious boyfriend that you killed your mother prior to his arrival.

> *(The two go around karate chopping the pillows while* **ILANA** *changes from chanclas to heels and refreshes her lipstick. Doorbell rings again.)*

Enrique. Fireplace!

> *(***ENRIQUE*** *turns on the fireplace.)*

We are nice normal people! Dammit! Smile and open the door.

> (**ENRIQUE** *takes a breath and puts a smile on his face.* **ILANA** *follows suit.* **ENRIQUE** *opens the door and there stands a white guy. He holds a star-shaped piñata and a bottle of wine.* **ENRIQUE** *exhales.*)

ENRIQUE. Can I help you?

MARCOS. Mr. Gomez?

ENRIQUE. Yes. Do I need to sign for these?

(To the **LADIES.***)* Who ordered a piñata?

YOLI. Marcos!

ENRIQUE. *(Not getting it.)* Marcos ordered a piñata?

> (**YOLI** *crosses to the door and kisses the white guy who we now know is* **MARCOS CRUISE**, *24. A long beat. Like...too long as* **ENRIQUE** *and* **ILANA** *take in what is happening.*)

YOLI. Guys?

ENRIQUE. <u>You're</u> Marcos?

MARCOS. *Sí. Mucho gusto, señor. Y, usted también, señora. Es un placer conocerlos.*

YOLI. Babe, you are so sweet but you don't have to speak Spanish.

MARCOS. *No, no. No hay problema. Tengo que practicar porque mi abuela está muy enojada conmigo porque dice que ahora mi Español no es muy bueno.*

YOLI. My mom doesn't speak it.

MARCOS. What?

YOLI. Spanish. She doesn't speak Spanish.

MARCOS. She doesn't?

(**ENRIQUE** *and* **ILANA** *both seem in a trance.*)

ENRIQUE. You're Marcos?

MARCOS. Indeed, I am.

ENRIQUE. Indeed he is. I'm just going to say it… You're a white guy.

YOLI. Dad!

ENRIQUE. What? He is!

YOLI. So are you! You're white.

ENRIQUE. Stop with that. No, I'm not!

YOLI. You are. You're Cuban and your grandparents came from Spain. You are white.

ENRIQUE. Not this again. Yoli.

YOLI. That is a fact. I can't say facts now?

ENRIQUE. *(To* **MARCOS**.*)* My daughter's new thing is to tell me that I'm a colonizer.

MARCOS. Oh, I'm a colonizer, too! Should we fist bump?

(**ENRIQUE** *laughs.*)

ENRIQUE. He's funny.

MARCOS. Thank you, sir. *Señor.* Sir.

ILANA. Come in, please.

MARCOS. This is for you.

>(*He hands* **ILANA** *the piñata and stick, and hands* **ENRIQUE** *the wine.* **ENRIQUE** *looks at it, not impressed.*)

ILANA. Uh, thank you?

>(**MARCOS** *nervously talks over them as they all move to the couch.*)

MARCOS. So the piñata... Let me explain. I went to buy wine and the store had these piñatas and I can see how that would seem random, but in the moment it seemed – I don't know, charming? A conversation starter? 'Cause, I'm sure you know, but I just found out the historical significance of the piñata and its origins in Spain.

(Blank stare from all.)

Oh, Oh, Oh, do you not know? Oh this is very exciting.

YOLI. He gets so excited by knowledge.

*(**ENRIQUE** and **ILANA** are still...stunned.)*

MARCOS. Okay, so, piñatas which are like...so Mexican, right? Or so we think! They were actually first traced back to Spain in the fourteenth century.

ILANA. Oh, how interesting.

MARCOS. And the seven points repped the seven deadly sins and the candies inside represented the riches of the kingdom of heaven, the colors represented the temptation to fall in with these sins and the stick is the virtue to fight the sins and the blindfold...is faith. How we have to believe even what we cannot see. Mexico's first documented piñata was hung at a church by these monks who were looking to put some Christianity in the Aztecs' December festival, which celebrated the birth of the Aztec god Huitzilopochtli [hweet-see-luh-powch-tuh-lee] – so, like, it was one of the first moments of the colonization of culture. Messed up, right? But also super interesting.

*(Nothing from **ILANA** and **ENRIQUE**.)*

YOLI. Wow. I didn't know that. Did you guys – I can tell from their faces that they didn't know that either. Thanks, babe.

MARCOS. Yeah, so I thought maybe after dinner it would be fun to play and eat the candy and have a story to tell at our – well, a story about the first time we met.

ENRIQUE. Oh we'll have a story to tell alright.

(A beat. It's awkward AF.)

So you are Mexican how exactly?

YOLI. Dad –

ENRIQUE. What?

YOLI. Mexicans come in all colors.

MARCOS. No, it's okay. I get asked this a fair amount, actually. Being named Marcos. Being born in Mexico. Being fluent in Spanish. Yeah, so, my parents Marty and Elaine Cruise –

ENRIQUE. Cruz?

MARCOS. C-R-U-I-S-E like a Tom. Not C-R-U-Z like a Ted. Yeah. Sorry about him. Don't know why I'm apologizing for him, but seems like white people are somehow to blame so, I'll take the hit. So, Marty and Elaine were both from outside of Boston, did a semester abroad and they just fell in love with *Mexico*. My mom changed her major to *Español* and my dad remained a business major, but finished his studies in *Mexico* City to be with her. Then I was born there and then we moved to *Los Angeles* when my dad got a job doing business relations with The Dodgers. So, I'm a dual citizen, but I can't run for President.

ENRIQUE. Oh, okay... So... That makes sense... You're not *really* Mexican.

MARCOS. No. I am.

ENRIQUE. No.

MARCOS. Yes. Culturally. Spiritually. Legally.

ENRIQUE. No.

MARCOS. My passport would disagree.

YOLI. *Papi.*

ENRIQUE. No! I went to Florence, Italy and fell in love with it. Doesn't make me *Italiano.*

YOLI. But you weren't born there. You didn't spend formative years there. You don't know the language fluently.

ENRIQUE. His Spanish is fine. Not great. Fine.

YOLI. It's better than Mom's!

ENRIQUE. *(Like it's an insult.)* Hey! Don't you speak about your mother like that.

ILANA. Enrique!

(To **MARCOS.***)* I'm so sorry, Marcos.

MARCOS. No, I think this makes for spirited conversation.

ILANA. You do?

YOLI. Yes. Marcos isn't afraid of hard conversations.

ENRIQUE. I'm not afraid of hard conversations.

YOLI. Well, Marcos can keep his temper through them.

ENRIQUE. Then definitely not Mexican.

YOLI. Cubans are worse!

ENRIQUE. *Carajo,* Yoli!

YOLI. Are you or are you not starting to raise your voice?

ENRIQUE. *(Raising his voice.)* No!

> *(***ENRIQUE** *tries to hold his temper, but it might give him an aneurism.)*

MARCOS. Babe, you have to be forgiving of your father's big feelings. Often aggressiveness is just a sign that someone is in distress, but doesn't have the tools to work through the moment calmly.

ENRIQUE. *(Furious.)* I have the tools!!

YOLI. Is it a blowtorch and a firearm? 'Cause that's what it's giving.

> **(MARCOS** *puts his hand on* **YOLI***'s knee. He's got it.)*

MARCOS. Have your feelings, Mr. Gomez. It's an honor to bear witness to your growth.

ENRIQUE. *Voy a matar a este chiquito!*

YOLI. He can understand you.

ENRIQUE. *Coño.*

YOLI. Dad, relax.

ILANA. Enrique, sit down and take a breath!

ENRIQUE. Everyone stop telling me what to do!

> *(A beat.)*

I'm going to sit down and take a breath.

(Sotto.) I have tools! I have tools.

ILANA. *(To* **MARCOS.***)* Our daughter's new thing is to push our buttons – But we're trying to roll with it.

YOLI. I'm not trying to push your buttons. I'm trying to have open and honest conversations with you guys and the man I love.

ENRIQUE. You love him now?

YOLI. I have loved him for awhile.

MARCOS. Love you, too, babe.

ENRIQUE. I just found out it was serious fifteen minutes ago! Now she loves him?

ILANA. I think it's great that she's in love.

(*To* **MARCOS**.) And this reaction is not about you, Marcos. I mean, we love white people. Some of our best friends are white. Anyway, lalalala... Let's get this train back on track.

(*There is a beat.*)

Why don't we hear the story of how you two met? That'll be nice.

YOLI. We actually first met, like, three years ago. I was briefly dating this guy Sebastian who was friends with Marcos.

MARCOS. Sebastian. Good guy. Cuban.

ENRIQUE. Like actually Cuban or a white guy who went to Cuba and bought a cigar once?

ILANA. Not helping.

ENRIQUE. No, I'm just trying to figure out if my daughter liking white guys parading as Latinos is a kink or –

YOLI. *Papi.* Stop.

MARCOS. Sebastian is Cuban from Cuba. His mother actually died on a raft while leaving Cuba so he was raised by his *tía* in Miami.

ENRIQUE. That's very sad. Well now I feel like a jerk.

YOLI. You said it.

ENRIQUE.	**ILANA**.
What did you say to me?	What did you say to your father?

YOLI. You said it!

MARCOS. Babe, don't. He's in pain.

ENRIQUE. Stop speaking for me, Marcos.

MARCOS. Of course. I realize how patronizing I must seem –

ENRIQUE. Seem??

YOLI. Dad, you need to chill.

ENRIQUE. Listen, young lady.

ILANA. Can we please fresh start? We have a guest? We have enchiladas!

MARCOS. Ooo, *enchiladas*!

        (**ENRIQUE** *gives him a death stare.* **ILANA** *hands him his drink.*)

ILANA. *(To* **MARCOS.***)* Yeah, 'cause this is not who we are. I'm so sorry things are so uncomfortable.

MARCOS. Oh, I'm not uncomfortable. While I acknowledge that the current vibe is heavy I feel light within the gravitas.

YOLI. I told them we had sex.

MARCOS. Ah. I see. Well, that explains it. Yes. We have made love. Yes. And I, personally, bristle at calling it "sex" 'cause that just feels so reductive of the, dare I say, spiritual experience that I feel making love with your daughter.

ENRIQUE. No, no, no, no, no! We are not talking about this in front of him.

YOLI. It's not a surprise to him. He was there.

MARCOS. I want you to know I always ask for consent and am committed and focused on your daughter's pleasure.

ENRIQUE. No. No. *Y* no. This is not appropriate. These are not things you talk about when you meet the parents.

ILANA. We can literally talk about anything else.

ENRIQUE. Your grandfather still thinks your mother is a virgin! It's called respect!

ILANA. Take a breath.

ENRIQUE. You need to be scared. Marcos, why aren't you scared?

MARCOS. You want me to be scared? I thought you wanted me to be comfortable.

ENRIQUE. She wants you to be comfortable. I want you to be scared. He should be scared, right?

ILANA. It is the polite thing to do.

MARCOS. Uh, I'm starting to feel a low level dread if that helps.

ENRIQUE. It doesn't help! It does not help.

(A beat.)

MARCOS. You guys seem like really nice people so – I'm not really feeling like my life is in danger or anything.

ENRIQUE. Let me tell you something. See in my day, I did feel like my life was in danger when I met the parents. Her father was 5'5" and I was scared shitless! I would have never been so casual and opinionated in front of my girlfriend's father.

YOLI. That's pretty old school, Dad.

ENRIQUE. Maybe. But I like it. I was looking forward to it.

(To **ILANA**.*)* And now he's robbing me of it.

MARCOS. I'm sorry? *Señor.* Sir. I'm just trying to be myself.

ENRIQUE. Well that's where you've gone wrong! When you meet the parents you have to put on a show. You have to have worried about this for days. You should have had a sleepless night. I want to be dazzled. Dazzle me, Marcos!

(To himself.) Talking about having sex with my –

MARCOS. *(Correcting.)* Making love.

(Off his look.) I just feel it's an important distinction so –

ENRIQUE. *(To **ILANA**, asking for help.)* He doesn't get it.

ILANA. I see that, baby.

ENRIQUE. Why doesn't he get it?

ILANA. I don't know. He should get it. We're gonna figure this out.

YOLI. She does this. Can't stand conflict.

ILANA. Hey! You need to chill out. You make it seem like I'm a freak 'cause I don't like conflict.

MARCOS. *(Trying to calm the moment.)* If there is anything I can do. I'd love to be a balm in this moment.

ILANA. You've done enough, Marcos.

ENRIQUE. I'd say too much. If you want to invent a time machine and go back in time so I can unhear what I've heard then – do that.

MARCOS. If I invented a time machine I'd like kill Hitler or something. Not sure I'd use it to –

ENRIQUE. Stop talking. Stop. Talking.

        *(**MARCOS** just nods.)*

MARCOS. *(Super fast.)* Can I just amend my last statement 'cause I don't think I'd kill Hitler. I mean, I'd want someone to kill Hitler, but I'm not a violent man. Like I couldn't pull the trigger. I just needed you guys to know that.

(Breath.) Okay, I'm done talking.

ENRIQUE. Is there blood dripping out of my ear? I'm seriously asking. I don't think I'm okay.

ILANA. You're fine. Everything is fine.

(To **YOLI.***)* You know it's okay to have a nice time, right? Not everything needs to be a deep exploration of humanity. Can we please just get this back on track and remember our manners?

YOLI. Mom, being polite and being kind are just forms of deceit.

ILANA. What?

YOLI. It's just society's way of ignoring problems.

ILANA. Maybe you are creating the problem where there was no problem!

MARCOS. If I may –

YOLI. Please, babe.

MARCOS. Your mother's body language is telling me you have hit a boundary. And that you need to back off for the moment.

YOLI. Well, I do want to be respectful of her boundaries.

ENRIQUE. What is happening?

ILANA. I don't know.

MARCOS. What would you like to talk about Mrs. Gomez?

ILANA. *(To* **MARCOS** *and* **YOLI.***)* I mean, I would love for you to finish the story of how you met. I think we got sidetracked.

MARCOS. Great. Yes. Let's do that.

YOLI. Okay.

MARCOS. Oh, well. The second time we met was like a year later in my Poli-Sci class. I was a senior and she was the only sophomore and she had the most insightful questions. Which caught my attention immediately – like who is this gorgeous girl saying all of these really smart things. And I was like I think that's that girl Sebastian was dating and I stupidly assumed that was still going on.

YOLI. It was long over.

MARCOS. Which I didn't know. And when I graduated I immediately did Teach for America post grad. But she would keep popping into my head.

YOLI. He was placed in a school outside of Detroit.

MARCOS. And since I'm fluent in Spanish, I was able to really connect with the Latino families. And I really saw firsthand how the climate crisis affected communities of color and thought I should get into environmental work. Which took me to Mexico City.

>   (**ILANA** *is dazzled.* **ENRIQUE** *not so much – he starts making snoring sounds.* **ILANA** *swats him.*)

YOLI. Where I was studying abroad.

MARCOS. And –

YOLI. So, it's a Friday and I'm in my final class before the weekend, and I happen to look out the window. I never look out the window during class. But for some reason I do. And who do I see walking outside... Marcos. And something in me told me to run out there. Class wasn't over and I grabbed my bag and ran outside –

MARCOS. And I was headed home from a meeting and took a wrong turn that took me down that street. I wasn't supposed to be there. I was lost. When I hear this angel call my name. I turned and there she was. And we kind of just...

YOLI. Stared at each other. And then we started laughing 'cause why were we staring at each other. But it felt like...I was finally home. Like...it was –

MARCOS. Magical.

YOLI. Yeah. And we have been pretty inseparable ever since.

>   (**ILANA** *is moved to tears.*)

ENRIQUE. Are you crying?

ILANA. Yes. It's a beautiful story.

ENRIQUE. Yes, to recap she saw him on the street and said his name.

ILANA. Stop it. That was a beautiful story thank you for telling it.

MARCOS. I'd love to hear how you two met. Enough about me. I'm pretty boring actually.

ENRIQUE. Finally we agree on something.

YOLI. Dad.

MARCOS. No. He's not wrong. Boring gets a bad rap, but boring doesn't give you cancer. Boring isn't excessive feelings that burst out in a chaotic rage. Boring can just mean peace.

ILANA. Peace is good.

ENRIQUE. *(To* **YOLI.***)* And you like this, Yoli? Someone that talks like a self help book?

MARCOS. *(Touched.)* Thank you.

ENRIQUE. It wasn't a compliment.

MARCOS. Well, I choose to receive it that way.

YOLI. Isn't he amazing? Marcos isn't afraid to ask questions and dig deeper. He isn't afraid to listen or be wrong. He sees it as an opportunity for growth. We talk about everything. He even goes to therapy.

ENRIQUE. So what? I went to therapy.

YOLI. Yeah, right!

ENRIQUE. No, I did.

ILANA. He did.

YOLI. What? After years of begging you went to therapy? And I'm just finding out now?

ENRIQUE. You've only been home for twenty-four hours. I was going to tell you but I've been a bit distracted. But, yes. I went.

YOLI. Wow. This is huge.

MARCOS. That's so great. Congratulations, Mr. Gomez.

ENRIQUE. Take it easy. Oooo, I talked to a person. I didn't win a medal in the Olympics.

ILANA. He doesn't like to boast.

YOLI. I'm both thrilled and also…curious. What finally made you go?

>   (**ILANA** *and* **ENRIQUE** *look at each other.* **ENRIQUE** *shrugs.*)

ILANA. He had a heart attack.

YOLI. WHAT?

ILANA. We didn't want to bother you.

YOLI. WHAT?

ILANA. See, you're upset and we didn't want to upset you. Look, he's fine now.

YOLI. Guys!

ENRIQUE. Relax. It was a little heart attack. I was only in the hospital for a day.

YOLI. You were in the hospital?

ENRIQUE. For one day. It was nothing. You were on Spring Break.

YOLI. I could have come home!

ENRIQUE. For what? Your generation really makes too much out of everything. It was no big deal. Everyone gets heart attacks. It was my turn.

ILANA. It really was very mild. He had some outpatient follow-up and his doctor said he needed to do something to manage his stress. So he prescribed therapy.

YOLI. And you're sure you're okay?

ENRIQUE. Never better. 'Til tonight.

YOLI. Oh my God. Dad! Okay, well, tell me about therapy.

ENRIQUE. I talked to the guy for an hour... I made him laugh, he took notes. At first it seemed like he actually may have gotten more out of it than I did. But then I had a breakthrough. He said my emotional outbursts can be healthy and it's good I get it all out. And I agreed. He suggested I do some cardio. And then the hour was up. Overall, it was positive. And I haven't had a heart attack since. So yeah I did it. I went to therapy and I am cured.

YOLI. Oh, you went once?

ENRIQUE. Yep.

YOLI. When was this?

ENRIQUE. Few months ago.

YOLI. Okay. Yeah, no. You gotta keep going.

ENRIQUE. What?

YOLI. Yeah, you go every week.

ENRIQUE. Why?

YOLI. To get to the bottom of it.

ENRIQUE. I did. I got to the bottom of it.

YOLI. No. You can't have. It takes years.

ENRIQUE. Maybe for some. Not for me.

ILANA. Your father has always been an overachiever.

MARCOS. Maybe he got everything he needed in that one session.

ENRIQUE. Thank you, Marcos.

YOLI. But he couldn't have.

ENRIQUE. But I did.

YOLI. No!

ILANA. Why are you upset that your father is healed?

YOLI. I'm not because he's not. You really think he's healed?

ILANA. Oh, you're a doctor now? Okay, that's enough. I get that you feel all empowered since graduating college. But you do not know everything!

YOLI. And neither do you.

ENRIQUE. Don't talk to your mother like that.

YOLI. Are you upset because I don't think you guys know everything?

ILANA. I thought my parents knew everything.

ENRIQUE. Me too.

YOLI. But they didn't.

ENRIQUE. Don't talk about your grandparents like that.

YOLI. I'm not saying you all aren't smart. But I also ain't calling *abuelo* to talk quantum physics. But if you think your parents knew everything and you think you know everything then it's no wonder you take issue with me challenging you about anything. Nobody knows everything!

ENRIQUE. We are good parents!

YOLI. You are fantastic parents!

MARCOS. She says that all of the time, by the way. She thinks you two are fantastic.

YOLI. Under the circumstances.

ILANA. What is that? Started as a compliment then –

ENRIQUE. Definitely turned into an insult. If you think we're such great parents then why do you keep attacking us?

YOLI. Two things can be true at the same time. I can think you are the greatest parents and also think that you are wrong about some stuff. I love you guys!

ILANA. Well you could lead with that.

YOLI. I just said it!

ILANA. No. You said

(*Overdramatic and childish.*) "I love you guys!"

That's not

(*Thoughtful and sweet.*) I love you guys.

YOLI. Mom.

ILANA. It's different.

MARCOS. She's not wrong.

(*This hits* **YOLI**.)

YOLI. Okay. Okay.

(*Sweetly.*) I love you guys.

ILANA. Oh, it's really life-giving to hear it that way.

YOLI. And I love that I can be myself here. I've never felt like I had to pretend to be something I'm not. But –

ILANA. Do we need to hear what comes after the "but"?

YOLI. I think it can be expansive to discuss further.

ILANA. Devil's Advocate: we had one child. You. And I'm not having any more kids. So, any notes or comments about how I could have done it better would really only be useful if I were going to do it again. And, as I've stated, I'm not. So, why would any further comments about how you were brought up be necessary?

ENRIQUE. She makes a good point.

YOLI. I guess...it would be for your own growth.

ILANA. I'm good. Like, if I made a great pie and it was the only pie I'd ever make, and you liked it but had thoughts...I'd say you could keep those to yourself because I'm not making another pie. Now, maybe you'll want to make pie one day. I hope you do. You can certainly take your thoughts and adjust the recipe when you make your pie. But hearing how I could have made a better pie is just ridiculous 'cause I already made it. I love the pie as is. So, all I need at this point is a "thank you" for making such a freaking amazing pie.

MARCOS. Well, let me be the one to thank you both then for making Yoli. 'Cause I think she's perfect. She is a wonderful pie. A delicious pie. So yummy.

ENRIQUE. I think we can lose the pie metaphor now.

(*A buzzer goes off.*)

ILANA. Oh, those are the enchiladas. I'm gonna go check on them. Enrique, why don't you join me?

(**ENRIQUE** *joins her.*)

We'll be right back.

(**ILANA** *and* **ENRIQUE** *cross off. A beat.*)

MARCOS. (*To* **YOLI**.) Ohmygod, I'm tanking this.

YOLI. No.

MARCOS. They hate me.

YOLI. No.

MARCOS. I brought a thirty dollar bottle of wine and a piñata. What was I thinking?

YOLI. Under normal circumstances I think it would have been an adorable conversation starter –

MARCOS. That was the plan! And then I was just so...me, wasn't I?

YOLI. Charming and interesting? Yes.

MARCOS. Your dad's not wrong... There is a code of conduct. I am entirely too comfortable and casual. One of the side effects of my white male privilege. I should have pretended to be afraid out of respect to your father.

YOLI. Don't let him get to you. This has nothing to do with you. Things were tense before you got here.

MARCOS. We did have a plan.

YOLI. We did.

MARCOS. So, I love you but I have to confront the fact that you said you were going to prep them about me and really hit home that we are the real thing.

YOLI. You're right. I got home and totally reverted. It's like your childhood home does something to you.

MARCOS. I feel that.

YOLI. Thank you. And I guess if I'm guilty of anything it's hubris that they'd be so excited to have me back and then they'd meet you and see how amazing you are and everything would be fine.

MARCOS. Taking me through it helps me understand you. Thank you for your honesty.

YOLI. Thank you for your understanding.

MARCOS. Should we breathe it out and shake it off?

YOLI. Yes, please.

> *(They both take deep breaths together then shake like they are getting bad vibes out of their bodies.)*

MARCOS. You good?

YOLI. I'm good.

MARCOS. Okay, so now that we are more centered – we need to come up with a new plan.

YOLI. Yes. But not for tonight.

MARCOS. I'm sensing some avoidance.

YOLI. I think the gentle thing to do would be to give them more time to get to know this adult me and get used to the idea of you. And then we can tell them. So, why don't I just call it.

MARCOS. I can turn this around.

YOLI. Babe, you have nothing to turn around. They're upset with me. You are just collateral damage...and white.

MARCOS. I just want to tell them tonight. I want to scream it from the rooftops!

YOLI. Trust me, tonight is not the night.

MARCOS. I hate secrets.

YOLI. I know. But sometimes secrets need to stay secrets to avoid blowing things up. I need more time and I need you to respect that.

MARCOS. I do respect that but I don't want that respect to turn into resentment.

YOLI. Okay, if there is an organic opening then we can tell them. If not, we do it next time. Fair?

MARCOS. Fair. God, I love you.

YOLI. I love you.

(Calling off.) Mami, I'm gonna show Marcos the gazebo.

ILANA. *(Offstage.)* Okay!

(They cross off over the following.)

MARCOS. Your parents have gazebo money? Maybe I should be more scared.

(As they re-enter, **ILANA** *and* **ENRIQUE** *chat in the hallway.)*

ILANA. We have to get our shit together now.

ENRIQUE. Is it me or is he not just white, but the whitest white guy. Like I can almost see through him.

ILANA. Who cares if he's white.

ENRIQUE. Can't she just date a real Mexican kid who I can talk cars and baseball with?

ILANA. You haven't even tried to talk cars or baseball with him. This is our only daughter. She has brought someone home and our job is to try to love him.

ENRIQUE. He don't know about cars.

ILANA. Really?

(Then.)

You have been the only man in her life and now you have to share her.

ENRIQUE. I just thought he'd be more –

ILANA. Like you?

(Then.)

Baby, if we want to stay in her life then we need to try to embrace this boy. Operation love up on Marcos. Try. Please?

*(***ILANA*** *goes in for a kiss. Her seduction works.)*

ENRIQUE. Okay.

(Then.)

Why are you so good to me?

ILANA. Because you're dynamite in the sack.

ENRIQUE. Oh yeah.

> *(She turns and he gives her a little smack on the butt. She smiles.)*

ILANA. Enchiladas need another twenty. But I have salad. So, let's eat!

> *(****ENRIQUE**** and ****ILANA**** reenter the room as ****YOLI**** and ****MARCOS**** come back inside.)*

MARCOS. Well, it smells amazing. I am honored that you cooked me some authentic enchiladas. Is it a family recipe?

YOLI. Uh-oh.

MARCOS. What?

ILANA. No. It's nothing. It's fine. I don't cook.

MARCOS. What?

ILANA. I don't cook. Not all women cook, Marcos.

MARCOS. Oh, I don't think all women should cook. But you said you made ench–

ENRIQUE. No, she said we had enchiladas.

ILANA. And he assumed I cooked them. Because why wouldn't he? It's fine. I hired these amazing chefs to prepare them and I put them in the oven. I meant to learn to cook but – I meant to do a lot of things and time moves very quickly and before you know it, you are an adult woman who can't speak Spanish or cook. Really being confronted with how short life is tonight.

> *(They all sit in a long and uncomfortable silence.)*

ENRIQUE. I'd like us to say grace. Am I going to get a lecture about that?

YOLI. No. I think prayer is lovely.

ENRIQUE. Well, thank God for that.

YOLI. Not sure I believe in God anymore, but definitely love sitting in gratitude over a meal.

ILANA. You don't have to say everything out loud. Just a suggestion.

ENRIQUE. In the name of the Father, and the Son and the Holy Spirit.

>(**ENRIQUE** *goes to grab* **ILANA** *and* **YOLI***'s hands. They all hold hands and say the prayer together. Even* **MARCOS** *knows it.)*

ALL. Bless us oh Lord in these thy gifts which we are about to receive from thy bounty through Christ our Lord, Amen.

>*(They all cross themselves.)*

ENRIQUE. *Salud.*

>*(They raise their glasses. Then begin eating. We sit for a moment in the tension.)*

You know the prayers. You Catholic?

>(**ENRIQUE** *takes a bite of his salad.)*

MARCOS. Aren't all Mexicans?

>(**ENRIQUE** *coughs then chokes on a grape in the salad. He coughs. It gets worse.)*

YOLI. Dad? You okay. Oh my god, he's choking.

ILANA. Arms up! I'll get him water.

MARCOS. I know the Heimlich maneuver!

ENRIQUE. No!

(**ENRIQUE** *gasps as he chokes but doesn't want* **MARCOS** *giving him the Heimlich maneuver.* **ILANA** *pours water.*)

ILANA. Enrique. Let him.

YOLI. Dad, what are you –

MARCOS. Please, Mr. Gomez. Let me –

YOLI. I can't believe you are being stubborn now!

ILANA. Honestly, Enrique!

MARCOS. It's okay. If he passes out I also know CPR and can give him mouth to mouth to resuscitate him.

*(Upon this news, **ENRIQUE** changes his tune.)*

ENRIQUE. No!

YOLI. Dad, just let him give you the Heimlich!

ENRIQUE. Okay.

MARCOS. Do I have your consent?

(**ENRIQUE** *rolls his eyes and nods.* **MARCOS** *gives him the Heimlich maneuver and dislodges a grape.*)

ENRIQUE. Oh my god.

MARCOS. Got it.

YOLI. Thank you, babe.

ILANA. Yes, thank you, Marcos.

MARCOS. Of course. Happy to help.

ENRIQUE. Help? I started choking in the first place because of you. You don't get to almost kill somebody and then take the credit for saving their life!

ILANA. Enrique. Calm down. Your heart.

(**ILANA** *gives him a look. He exhales deeply.*)

ENRIQUE. Thank you.

MARCOS. My pleasure. I mean, not my pleasure – I didn't enjoy – Thank you. You're welcome.

> (*They all sit and resume eating the salad. An awkward beat.* **MARCOS** *downs his full glass of wine. Then he refills the glass with the decanter. After another beat…*)

ILANA. Now, let me tell you about this salad because I <u>did</u> make it and I'm very proud of it. Packed with veggies, cotija cheese. And grapes. So a little sweet and a little salty. Plus, tortilla chips of course. Crumbled up in there. Buen appetit-o.

> (*There is a beat. Everyone chews. Some MMM sounds.*)

MARCOS. Really a taste explosion. Is that a toasted pepita?

ILANA. It is!

MARCOS. What a nice surprise.

ILANA. I'm glad you all like it. Look at that. Order restored by a salad. See, this is more like who we are. We're a loving family.

ENRIQUE. We are. So, Marcos, so that I can better understand – you really think you're Mexican?

MARCOS. I do.

ILANA. My love, I think we've moved past this.

ENRIQUE. No, my love, I think we need to clear it up to move past it. Yoli wants us to have the hard conversations so let's do that. Shall we?

MARCOS. Hard to say no to that.

> (**ILANA** *exhales.*)

ENRIQUE. *(To* **MARCOS.***)* Great. So you feel Mexican because you were born there?

MARCOS. Yes. Where were you born?

ENRIQUE. Here.

MARCOS. And do you identify as American?

(A beat.)

YOLI. Interesting.

ILANA. Now for the dressing… It's an avocado ranch made from scratch. Not by me. But I bought it at the farmer's market where someone did make it from scratch. Really completes the salad I think.

ENRIQUE. I do consider myself American. Yes.

MARCOS. So you get it.

(To **ILANA.***)* The dressing really is terrific, Mrs. Gomez. So creamy.

ILANA. That's greek yogurt. So, half the fat of sour cream. Delicious and nutritious. And, please, call me Ilana.

MARCOS. Okay, Ilana.

ENRIQUE. Still don't get it, Marcos. But I am trying.

ILANA. Trying is the important part.

MARCOS. Well, Mr. Gomez – Enrique –

ENRIQUE. No. I'd like for you to call me Mr. Gomez.

ILANA. Enrique!

ENRIQUE. It's a sign of respect. Let him call you what you want, I like Mr. Gomez.

YOLI. He doesn't like it. It makes him feel like an old man which is sort of how he is behaving.

ILANA. Yoli.

YOLI. He always tells people to call him Enrique. Actually, he usually says "call me Rick." To further anglo-cize himself.

ILANA. Stop it.

ENRIQUE. I don't try to anglo-cize myself.

ILANA. Okay, you two, enough.

ENRIQUE. We're not doing this again. You are not the Latino police, Yoli.

YOLI. I just don't want you guys to sound like out of touch old people who don't understand how the world works.

ENRIQUE. Oh, and you understand how the world works?

YOLI. I think I do. Like, Mom identifies as Mexican and Puerto Rican but she wasn't born in Mexico or Puerto Rico. She was born here. And you identify as Cuban but you weren't born there either. You've never even been to Cuba.

ENRIQUE. What's your point.

YOLI. You aren't Cuban.

ENRIQUE. Excuse me?

YOLI. You're Cuban American and Mom, you aren't Puerto Rican and Mexican. You are Puerto Rican and Mexican American.

MARCOS. *(To* **ILANA.***)* Oh yeah, in Mexico they definitely wouldn't say you're Mexican.

ENRIQUE. Oh, so you're Mexican and she's not?

ILANA. Baby, I got this. My father's side was born on this land. Six generations. Pasadena was Mexico! I have documents from the early 1800s tracing my family line back to the Tongva and the Figueroas. California was annexed in 1848. We were here before that. So I was born in Mexico! It's just not called that anymore.

YOLI. See, complicated history makes for complicated identity.

MARCOS. Wow, that's a cool story.

ILANA. Well, that "cool story" sucked for my family to live.

(This shuts everyone down.)

MARCOS. I'm sorry. I didn't mean –

YOLI. It's okay, baby. This is good.

ILANA. It is?

YOLI. Yes. Mom, I've never heard you talk about that before.

ILANA. Yeah, because it's awful. I don't understand why you like to talk about awful things.

YOLI. It's not that I like to it's that only talking about good things doesn't make bad things go away. I'd argue that so many problems that we currently are facing are because people don't know their history.

ENRIQUE. I don't know why we have to regurgitate everything that has happened to our people in the last two thousand years in order for us to have a conversation!

YOLI. We don't have to always talk about it but we <u>never</u> talk about it.

ILANA. So if we talk about it tonight can we never talk about it again?

ENRIQUE. She wants to talk about it? Then let's talk about it. We can start with your boyfriend who walked in here saying he's Mexican when he's white.

MARCOS. I was born and raised in Mexico! I am Mexican! I get that most of the world sees me as "white" whatever that is. What does white even mean? Skin color? If anything I'm peach.

ILANA. I've been called white. And Hispanic. Mexicana. Chicana. Boriqua. Latina. Latinx. I hate all of those. And I never really connected with any of them. I'm a mom! A wife. A boss. But Latinx? What is that?

ENRIQUE. Ugh, Latinx. Hate it.

YOLI. It's to be more inclusive.

ENRIQUE. And I try to be respectful of that even though I don't quite get it but, what? We have to change a whole word because one person might not identify that way? I mean, come on.

ILANA. Well, wait a minute. I don't love Latinx either but as things currently stand if there are ninety-nine women in a room it's Latinas but if one man enters we all suddenly become Latinos for that one man. How is this any different?

ENRIQUE. Wow. That's a good point. I never thought of it that way.

YOLI. Oh, is positive discourse happening?

ENRIQUE. Maybe. Maybe. Relax.

> *(Then.)*

But the "x." Hate the "x." And it doesn't translate when you speak Spanish.

YOLI. That's why I prefer the latest inclusive term… *Latine*. With an "e." Works in Spanish and English and it has no gender. You know, Spanish is such a gendered language, but *estudiante* is without gender.

MARCOS. *(To **ILANA**.) Estudiante* means student.

ILANA. Yes, thank you.

ENRIQUE. Well, I've been Latino or Cubano my whole life and I like it. I like the "o" – It feels good on me. I want to stay Latino.

YOLI. And you can stay Latino. It's about making a more inclusive word when referring to a group.

ENRIQUE. Oh, really?

YOLI. Yeah. You stay Latino. My whole thing is people getting cranky because "we're making up a word" like, do they not know all words were made up? And English today isn't Shakespeare's English – we morph. It's part of life. Part of growth. That we hopefully evolve into something better. And I do think Latine does that.

ENRIQUE. I don't hate Latine for a group – if I can stay Latino we're cool.

YOLI. Deal.

> *(They shake hands! A moment of peace. Then...)*

ILANA. You know, if I'm honest, I've never felt like I was Latina enough. I was never Mexican enough, never Puerto Rican enough, never brown enough, never American enough. People say, "you're 'ambiguous'" like it's a compliment. What is that? It's kinda like being told you're nothing. And that sucks. The only place I ever felt like I belonged was with my family.

YOLI. I'm so glad I get to teach you this stuff.

> *(**ILANA** and **ENRIQUE** do a double take.)*

ENRIQUE. She thinks she's teaching us stuff.

ILANA. I heard. It's adorable.

ENRIQUE. Do you really think we've never talked about any of this before? We have. And not only that we've lived through it. Talking only does so much. At some point you gotta get on with it and live your life.

YOLI. You may have talked about it but you've never talked about it with me.

ILANA. Maybe 'cause we hoped we wouldn't have to.

YOLI. Well, I like hearing what you think.

ENRIQUE. Alright, well, I think the whole melting pot thing really messes us up. Like we are all here from different places and we'll all just melt together. But I worry we lose something in that melting. My Anglo friends are all disconnected from their history. It's like to become American you have to shed your old skin and become this new thing.

ILANA. What if we could be like my salad instead? Each thing is still what it is, but together it makes something really wonderful.

ENRIQUE. How do we do that *mi amor*? 'Cause that's not what happens here. What we have done since the beginning of these United States is recruit new people, willingly or unwillingly, into this uniquely American idea that being a real American is being white. You've heard the phrase "All American"? What does that mean? Blonde hair and blue eyes. California girl? Blonde hair blue eyes...and a tan. When you say California girl you should think native woman... That is more accurate, like your mom said. But it's not what anybody thinks of. Being American means being white. And I worry Latinos are America's next white people. Look what it did to Marcos.

MARCOS. Wait, what did it do to me?

ENRIQUE. Where is your family from Marcos?

MARCOS. Mexico.

ENRIQUE. But where were they *really* from before Mexico.

MARCOS. Boston.

ENRIQUE. Before Boston?

MARCOS. Oh, uh, Germany, I think. Some British in there. A little Polish.

ENRIQUE. But you don't really know.

MARCOS. I don't.

ENRIQUE. That is sad. No wonder you are so excited about being Mexican. You're dying for some culture because you no longer have any of your own. You don't walk with the stories of your German ancestors or your Polish ancestors or your English ancestors as part of the fabric of who you are.

MARCOS. I don't.

ENRIQUE. Do you do any traditional things to honor those cultures?

MARCOS. *(Realizing.)* We do Mexican things.

ENRIQUE. So no. When your family became American, your true ancestry melted away. It got erased. And yet, every immigrant who first comes to this country starts as "the other" – Look at the Irish – there were actual signs on stores that said "No dogs. No Irish." But now… Irish are seen as "white people." Now there are parades. Now we drink green beer and we're all Irish on one day a year. We're one *Cinco de Mayo* away from being another American party where people drink margaritas and hit piñatas and don't know why and I don't want that.

    (He lets this land.)

So, that's why I guess I'm having a big reaction to you, Marcos. Because I was expecting somebody that looked like me. And I want my grandchildren to look like me. I'm not saying it's rational. And I'm not saying it's right. But it's how I feel. I don't want to be erased.

    (Beat.)

ILANA. You see. Therapy.

    (Then.)

Now, at the risk of you making fun of me I'd love it if we could change the subject to something a little lighter.

MARCOS. I agree.

YOLI. You do?

MARCOS. Yeah. It's good to let big conversations marinate. It's in the marinating that the juices break down the meat... Sometimes letting things sit is as important as the conversation itself.

ENRIQUE. That is the first smart thing you've said, Marcos.

YOLI. Now, why did you have to make that a dig?

ENRIQUE. What dig? I'm complimenting him.

YOLI. By telling him everything he said prior was stupid.

ENRIQUE. Everything he said prior WAS stupid. I'm embracing this honesty you are so passionate about.

MARCOS. Babe, it's fine. I take it as a compliment, sir.

ILANA. Fresh start.

(*Then.*)

Marcos, you a car guy?

MARCOS. I'd consider myself a bit of a motor head, yeah.

ENRIQUE. Uh ha. And what do you drive? A Prius?

MARCOS. A '67 Mustang Shelby GT 500 Fastback actually.

ENRIQUE. Shut up.

MARCOS. No, I do. It's outside.

ENRIQUE. You drive a '67 Shelby?

MARCOS. Yeah. I replaced the engine with a 5.0, but I'm looking for ways to make it run on solar. Not sure if Yol told you but I work for a solar company. I'm really fascinated by engines. Last week I got to look at a Waverly Electric.

YOLI. It's like a different language is being spoken.

ILANA. Well, I don't speak this one either.

ENRIQUE. Guys, a Waverly Electric was the first electric car ever invented.

MARCOS. Back in 1896.

YOLI. They had the ability to made electric cars back then?

MARCOS. Oh yeah but – they were expensive, the charge was low and ultimately gas –

ENRIQUE. – Big oil –

MARCOS. – shut down R&D.

ENRIQUE. Wow. I'm impressed.

MARCOS. Really? Well, if you want to drive the Shelby around later, you are welcome to.

ENRIQUE. I'd actually love that.

(A beat.)

MARCOS. I hear you're also a Dodgers fan?

ENRIQUE. Indeed I am.

MARCOS. Go Blue!

YOLI. Look at you two.

MARCOS. Baseball! One season, one game, one player even can bring people together like nothing else.

ENRIQUE. There was this twenty-year-old Mexican kid –

ENRIQUE.	**MARCOS**.
Fernando Valenzuela!	Fernando Valenzuela!

MARCOS. Did you see Valenzuela play?

ENRIQUE. Sure did.

> *(**ENRIQUE** mimics how Valenzuela used to pitch and **MARCOS** mirrors him. The two throw a pitch and off of the high **MARCOS***

tries to high five **ENRIQUE.** *But* **ENRIQUE** *does not return it.)*

MARCOS. That is epic. I'm so jealous.

ENRIQUE. See, Yol, we don't have to argue about everything.

ILANA. Seems you two have a lot in common.

ENRIQUE. You know what? I am gonna pull out the Château Haut-Brion.

ILANA. You've been saving that.

ENRIQUE. I have. I'd been saving it for a special occasion and what is more special than our wonderful daughter being home and introducing us to the new man in her life who drives a '67 Shelby.

> *(Everyone smiles. Okay. Things are finally going well.* **ENRIQUE** *pulls the bottle out from a special spot. He dusts it off and uncorks it. And begins to pour* **MARCOS** *a glass. Then* **ILANA.** *Then* **YOLI.** *Then himself over the following.)*

MARCOS. We actually do have something pretty major to celebrate.

YOLI. No.

MARCOS. What do you mean, no? This is an organic opening.

YOLI. No. Not an organic opening. Not an organic opening at all. The night just took a nice turn so maybe we just ride that wave and enjoy and we'll talk about other things on another night.

ILANA. What other things?

YOLI. Nothing.

ENRIQUE. Yoli, what's going on?

YOLI. Nothing.

MARCOS. Not nothing. Something. And I just bonded with your dad and this feels like the right moment.

ENRIQUE. Right moment for what?

YOLI. This is a bad idea.

MARCOS. Well, they know something is up. Can't put the toothpaste back in now. We gotta tell them.

ILANA. Yoli – what is he talking about?

YOLI. Don't be mad.

ENRIQUE. What the hell is going on, Yoli?

ILANA. I feel like I'm going to throw up. Tell us. What is going on.

YOLI. No it's good news. It's good 'cause Marcos and I are married! Surprise!

MARCOS. Yayyyyyy.

    (**ILANA** *and* **ENRIQUE** *both freeze.*)

ENRIQUE. What?   **ILANA.** WHAT??

ILANA. I can't feel my face.

ENRIQUE. My chest is on fire.

    (**YOLI** *pulls the necklace out of her shirt showing the ring.* **MARCOS** *pulls his ring out of his pocket.*)

MARCOS. I'm so happy to put this back on.

(He puts his ring back on.) I'm your son-in-law!

ENRIQUE. I'm going to kill you.

    (**ENRIQUE** *dashes toward* **MARCOS** *and* **ILANA** *and* **YOLI** *hold him back.*)

That's my baby! She's a child bride!

YOLI. Dad. I'm twenty-two.

ENRIQUE. No! No! No! No! You come to me! You ask <u>me</u> for her hand! *(Catching himself.)* Us. I caught it. Okay? I caught it. <u>Us.</u> You ask us for her hand. He's supposed to do that. We're supposed to meet him and then suss him out. He's supposed to be scared! Then over time maybe we grow to like him. MAYBE! Then he asks. You didn't ask us.

MARCOS. I'm sorry.

ENRIQUE. We just found out it was serious!!

YOLI. Mom, is he okay?

ILANA. I don't know if I'm okay.

ENRIQUE. He didn't ask!

ILANA. I know, baby.

ENRIQUE. He skipped the steps.

ILANA. I know!

ENRIQUE. He took a shortcut!

ILANA. Oh – He's making U-turns! He's not wearing a seatbelt! It's all a disaster!

(**ENRIQUE** *can't stop pacing.*)

ENRIQUE. I need to...scream? Punch someone? Hit something?

(**ENRIQUE** *and* **ILANA** *are gobsmacked and pacing. They don't know what to do.* **ILANA** *gets an idea. She grabs the piñata and the stick. She holds it up. Then she hands it to* **ENRIQUE**.*)*

ILANA. Hit it.

ENRIQUE. What?

ILANA. Everything you are feeling...take it out on this piñata!

(He nods and takes the stick. He begins to hit the piñata like it killed his mom.)

(Everyone watches until he stops. Out of breath. Tears in his eyes.)

ENRIQUE. That helped. Thank you, baby.

(She takes the stick from him and beats the crap out of the piñata. Candy is everywhere. The two hug. They look at each other, a beat. What the hell is happening. This is crazy! Then they start laughing.)

*(**MARCOS** and **YOLI** don't know what to make of it.)*

YOLI. I think I broke them.

*(**ILANA** and **ENRIQUE** laugh even harder.)*

ENRIQUE. She's married?! What??

ILANA. We're gonna save a fortune on the wedding 'cause it happened and we weren't invited!

(They both keep laughing.)

YOLI. Yes! Laughter is good.

ILANA. Where will you live?

YOLI. Here. With you.

*(They laugh even harder. Then...once the shock leaves their bodies the grief sets in. **ILANA** starts to cry. **ENRIQUE** adapts and holds her.)*

ENRIQUE. You've really upset your mother.

YOLI. Mami –

ILANA. No. You've talked a lot since you've been home. And I've let you. I've defended you. But this...this is cruel. You're our only daughter. You know how much your wedding day would mean to me. Us. Us, I caught it. And you cut us out of the most important day of your life? No. This I can't forgive, Yoli.

(*DING.*)

And those are the fucking enchiladas!

ENRIQUE. Totally forgot about dinner.

ILANA. I've lost my appetite. But you all should eat it. It's very good.

MARCOS. I'm really sorry that this was all such a surprise.

ILANA. A surprise is something fun! "Hey we're going to Disneyland!" That's a surprise. This is a shock! "Hey, you have to have an emergency rectal exam." That's what this feels like!

MARCOS. For the record, I wanted her to call you guys. Not to throw her under the bus, but I wanted her to tell you. To bless this.

ENRIQUE. I wouldn't have.

ILANA. I would have. I would have done anything to be included.

MARCOS. I'm so sorry. We just got carried away. We were on this beach in Rosarito, just out for a picnic and there was this family sitting next to us. And they were playing Uno and laughing. I just looked at her and knew I wanted all of that with her. I was overcome with this feeling and the words just flew out of my mouth. It was a surprise to me. I didn't have a ring or anything. It wasn't planned. And she said yes. And then she said "how about right now?" And we drove to a courthouse in San Diego. And it was kinda...perfect.

ENRIQUE. So to recap, he saw people playing Uno...and decided to ruin our daughter's future.

MARCOS. I'm a good guy, Mr. and Mrs. Gomez. I have a good job and I'm not afraid of hard work. So, if you can try and give me a shot...I won't let you down. I love your daughter very much and I just want to make her happy.

ILANA. All we want is her happiness. But, I don't know if I can get over this. I just don't know if I can. My heart is broken. You broke my heart.

ENRIQUE. *(To* **YOLI.***) Ven aquí!, Yoli. ¿Qué pasó?*

YOLI. *No sé.*

ENRIQUE. *¿Qué estabas pensando?*

YOLI. *No estaba pensando. Estaba sintiendo.*

ENRIQUE. *Ay dios.*

YOLI. I'm sorry, *mami.* I wasn't thinking. If I knew this is how you were gonna feel, I wouldn't have done it. I feel terrible.

ILANA. You should feel terrible. Because however bad you feel, is a sliver compared to the dagger I feel in my chest.

ENRIQUE. We're not like some estranged family that doesn't talk. We are – were – a close family.

YOLI. Are. We <u>are</u> close.

ILANA. Could have fooled me.

ENRIQUE. Why keep us from one of the most important days in your life?

YOLI. Do you have any idea what it's like to be raised in such a warm and loving home where your parents are so supportive and your family has sacrificed everything so that you can be anything you want to be?

*(*ILANA *and* ENRIQUE *are confused.)*

ILANA. I can't tell if that is a compliment or an insult.

ENRIQUE. I think it's supposed to be an insult when it should be a thank you.

YOLI. You guys don't get it. All I heard my whole life was about how hard it's been for our family so that I could be whatever I wanted to be. And I'm grateful. I'm so grateful I had no struggle. You guys all did it so I wouldn't have to. But...that means I have to be the best. My ancestors literally died so that I could be the best. I can't mess it up. I can't let you down. I have to be their wildest dreams or I'm worthless.

ILANA. Baby! Nobody thinks that.

YOLI. But I feel it. I've felt it in my body my whole life. I have to be the perfect kid. The perfect student 'cause I have no excuse. I can't let everyone down. You know there is this study they did on mice. Where they kept them in a box and every time they tried to leave they would shock them. So they stopped leaving the box. Then when those mice had babies they took those babies and put them in a different box away from their parents...and those mice, without knowing what happened to their parents, never left the box. They never saw it but it was in their bodies. It's the perfect representation of intergenerational trauma and how we pass it down. So, I want to be perfect for you but I'm not. I screw up! And I don't want to keep secrets from you but I also don't know how to navigate making mistakes and disappointing not just you but everyone who came before. But trust me when I say this isn't a disappointment. This is good.

ENRIQUE. *(To* **ILANA.***)* She didn't have a quinceañera. And I let that go. I said fine 'cause I was supposed to get that dance at her wedding.

ILANA. And I was supposed to plan a shower and help her pick out a wedding dress and make favors! But it's done. And as sad as I am about it – what can we do? Like, let's be real… We can't be upset with her forever. We love her. We're hurt because we love her. We can't be those people that allow our anger to consume us and it just drives more of a wedge. And that means we have to get okay with this. We need to get things back on track. Because we are the grown-ups and we don't want to be excluded from anything ever again.

ENRIQUE. I didn't get my dance!

(**ILANA** *gets an idea.*)

ILANA. I know. But that we can fix. Let's do it now.

ENRIQUE. What?

(**ILANA** *grabs her phone and a gentle acoustic ballad begins – just guitar and voice. Something like "Hold Me Now" by Lena Hall or "Anything for You" by Irene Diaz.* She takes **YOLI***'s hand and puts in into* **ENRIQUE***'s hand. And the two dance. It's lovely. He spins her, they start to enjoy it and with every move they heal. Then he pulls her in from behind and places his hand on her stomach in a dance move but she pulls away and widens her eyes. He looks at her and realizes.*)

No.

---

*A license to produce *One of the Good Ones* does not include a performance license for "Hold Me Now" or "Anything for You." The publisher and author suggest that the licensee contact ASCAP or BMI to ascertain the music publisher and contact such music publisher to license or acquire permission for performance of the song. If a license or permission is unattainable for "Hold Me Now" or "Anything for You," the licensee may not use the songs in *One of the Good Ones* but should create an original composition in a similar style or use a similar song in the public domain. For further information, please see the Music and Third-Party Materials Use Note on page iii.

YOLI. *Papi.*

ENRIQUE. *Dios mio.*

> (**ILANA**, *noticing they stopped, stops the music.)*

ILANA. Why did you stop?

(The doorbell rings.)

ENRIQUE. Are we expecting someone?

ILANA. No.

> *(The doorbell rings again.* **ILANA** *opens the door and sees* **PEDRO**.*)*

Oh, *Señor. Hola.* This is the flower guy. He doesn't speak English –.

PEDRO. *(In perfect English.)* I speak English.

ILANA. What?

PEDRO. Yeah. So I think I left my phone here.

ILANA. You speak English?

PEDRO. Yep. I was retracing my steps and I thought maybe when you went to get me that *"agua"* –

ILANA. You said you didn't speak English.

PEDRO. No. You never asked. You just assumed that I didn't and I went with it.

ILANA. So you just let me babble on, Pedro?

PEDRO. It's Pete actually.

ILANA. Well, Pete. That was not a nice thing to do. You let me think you spoke Spanish.

PEDRO. I do speak Spanish.

ILANA. Yes, but you let me think you only speak Spanish.

PEDRO.   Lady. Come on. I could tell you were a rich white-ina *(Pronounced "whytina" like "Latina.")* that was gonna be all weird, and I was right, so it was just easier to let you assume what you assumed so I could get out of here and likely you'd overtip out of guilt, which you did.

ILANA. White-ina? Well, now I want my tip back.

YOLI. Mom.

PEDRO. What?

ILANA. That's right. I want it back, Pete.

ENRIQUE. She doesn't. It's fine.

ILANA.   Don't speak for me, Enrique! I gave that tip thinking he was –

PEDRO. Poor and uneducated? So, you only tip when you feel sorry for people?

ILANA. No!

YOLI. I'll have you know she always tips really well.

PEDRO. I just want my phone. I don't want to get into it with a weird Latino family.

YOLI. Latine.

PEDRO. What?

YOLI. *Latine –*

PEDRO. Oh, you're one of those.

YOLI. One of what?

PEDRO. It doesn't matter. Did I bring pretty flowers? Yes. Did I place them at their desired location at the time they were expected? Yes. Seems like I did my job. And whatever weird situation I walked in on – I don't need to know any more about.

MARCOS. *Escucha, ellos son buena gente. Han estado bajo mucha presión pero –*

PEDRO. Take it easy, white guy. I don't actually care.

ENRIQUE. For your information, that white guy is Mexican – as Mexican as you are!

MARCOS. *(Too touched.)* Thank you.

PEDRO. Well, I don't know what that means since I'm Guatemalan. Listen, I got my phone. I'm not returning the tip. *Buenas Noches.*

(**PEDRO** *exits.)*

MARCOS. Did you mean that, Mr. Gomez? You finally see me as Mexican?

ENRIQUE. No. But I understand that you identify that way and that your passport says that. For tonight that's going to have to be enough.

MARCOS. I'll take it. Baby steps.

ENRIQUE. Speaking of – Yoli –

ILANA. Oh, right. You were going to say something.

YOLI. No, I wasn't.

ENRIQUE. Yoli. *Cuéntale la verdad a tu madre. Yo lo sé.*

YOLI. *¿Sabes qué?*

ENRIQUE. Yoli.

YOLI. *Papi, por favor no lo digas. Él no sabe.*

ILANA. Don't you dare speak Spanish right now!

MARCOS. Wait, am I *él?* What do I not *sabe?*

ENRIQUE. Wait, he doesn't know? You can't be serious. You have to tell them.

YOLI. Dad.

ENRIQUE. What? What?

YOLI. Give me a second.

ILANA. Guys?

ENRIQUE. *Tienes que decirle sobre el bebé! Ahora!*

ILANA. I know that word! Drink! And no, I don't need a drink. I just want to know what's going on.

ENRIQUE. *Beber* is drink. *Bebé* means –

MARCOS. Baby.

ILANA. No.

> *(Then.)*

Well, it all makes sense now.

MARCOS. Wait –?

ILANA. Yoli.

> **(ILANA** *rushes to hug her* **DAUGHTER.** *The two hug and cry.)*

I knew there was something. I knew. A mother always knows.

> *(She kisses and hugs* **YOLI.** *The two laugh through tears.)*

MARCOS. What is happening??

ILANA. She's pregnant!

YOLI. We're having a baby.

MARCOS. Wait, what?

> **(ILANA** *and* **ENRIQUE** *hug* **YOLI.)**

ILANA. Sit. Sit. How far along?

YOLI. Thirteen weeks.

MARCOS. Thirteen weeks?

YOLI. I've only known for sure for two weeks. And I wanted to come home to see my gyno who confirmed yesterday. They say strong heartbeat.

MARCOS. You've known for two weeks and you didn't tell me?

YOLI. I wanted to come home. To see my doctor. To see my parents.

MARCOS. That is not cool. That is not chill!

YOLI. I'm sorry. I was gonna tell you on the beach that day and then you proposed and I was just so happy that you wanted to marry me for me and not because you felt you had to. And it was like...perfect! I'm not coming home as some unwed pregnant daughter. We're married! I fixed it! We're coming home as a family!

>*(Then.)*

I have the pictures.

ILANA. I want to see the pictures!!

>*(**YOLI** gets up.)*

Sit down.

YOLI. The pictures. In my purse.

ILANA. Enrique, get her purse.

ENRIQUE. Marcos, get her purse.

>*(**MARCOS**, in a daze, goes to the purse and hands it to **ENRIQUE**, who hands it to **YOLI**.)*

So, this is why you really came home. This is why you've been hounding us.

ILANA. This is why you've been intensely questioning our parenting. Because you <u>are</u> making a pie!

YOLI. So, we're okay? I was so worried.

ILANA. Baby we're more than okay.

MARCOS. Ugh, we're not okay! What the hell, Yoli?!?

ENRIQUE. Marcos, lower your voice!

MARCOS. I'm gonna be a dad?

(**YOLI** *shows* **MARCOS** *the ultrasound.*)

YOLI. Yes.

MARCOS. Now don't get me wrong 'cause I'm happy about this but, like, you gotta let me freak out a little 'cause we have no secrets and you keep this <u>huge</u> one from me!

YOLI. I know.

MARCOS. I had a plan. And this was totally in it but like five years from now. So, I'm kinda flipping out 'cause I know the kind of dad I want to be and can I be that dad now? I mean, I guess I'll have to figure it out but wow...lots of big feelings.

ENRIQUE. It is an honor to bear witness to your journey, Marcos.

MARCOS. I know you're being sarcastic Mr. Gomez, but those words are a comforting ointment.

(*Then.*)

(*To* **ILANA** *and* **ENRIQUE**.) Wow. Just wow.

(**ILANA** *picks up the stick and hands it to* **MARCOS**.)

ILANA. Hit the piñata.

MARCOS. I don't think I need to resort to violence in this moment. I have other tools in my tool box –

ILANA. Hit the piñata, Marcos. It'll make you feel better. We've all freaked out a bit tonight. Welcome to the family.

(**ILANA** *grabs the stick and holds it out to* **MARCOS**. **MARCOS** *takes it and gives the piñata a tap.*)

ENRIQUE. Come on, Marcos. Colonize that piñata. Pay tribute to your ancestors.

(**MARCOS** *hits it a bit harder.*)

YOLI. Come on, baby. Let it all out!

(**MARCOS** *hits the piñata harder. And harder and harder. It does feel good. He hands the stick back to* **ENRIQUE** *and* **ENRIQUE** *goes in for a hug.*)

MARCOS. Thank you, Mr. Gomez.

ENRIQUE. You can call me, Enrique.

(**MARCOS** *gets emotional.*)

Are you crying?

MARCOS. No, Enrique.

(*Then.*)

Yeah. Maybe.

ENRIQUE. It's back to Mr. Gomez.

YOLI. Marcos, I'm so sorry. I promise I will never keep a secret from you ever again. I was just so scared.

MARCOS. And I hold space for that, but also have to hold space for my own pain at being left out of hearing our baby's heartbeat.

ENRIQUE. I remember when we first heard Yoli's heartbeat.

ILANA. We were terrified. And then suddenly we hear this boom ba-boom, ba-boom, ba-boom. And I saw the moment he knew he loved you already. And I knew it because I felt it, too.

(**ENRIQUE** *is moved and teary. He tries to hide it.*)

MARCOS. Are you crying?

ENRIQUE. It's allergies.

(**ILANA** *hands* **ENRIQUE** *a tissue.*)

YOLI. You guys! All I wanted was for this night to end with no more secrets and everyone on the same page and we did it! It's a miracle.

ENRIQUE. So to recap, Marcos went from boyfriend, to serious boyfriend, to husband, to father of my grandchild in under ninety minutes. And somehow I didn't kill him. That is a miracle.

ILANA. I think we have the piñata to thank. Ended up being a good idea after all. Now who wants candy?

(*They all raise their hands.* **ILANA** *takes a bunch of candy and lays an assortment on the table. They each get candy.*)

I get to plan a shower! You got your dance and I get my shower. I knew we could get back on track! Uh, so much to do! We'll need to put together a registry. Oh, and names!

YOLI. Oh, I already have the perfect name.

MARCOS. You do?

ILANA. Tell us.

YOLI. (*So excited.*) Açai. (*Ah-sah-ee.*)

(*Beat.*)

ENRIQUE. Like the bowl?

ILANA. She's kidding.

YOLI. I'm not.

ENRIQUE. You're seriously naming our grandchild after a tasteless purple mush.

YOLI. It's a superfood!

ENRIQUE.	**ILANA.**	**MARCOS.**
No, no *y* no.	What about Cecelia after your grandmother?	I feel like I should have a say in this…

(Suddenly, smoke starts to waft in from the kitchen.)

ENRIQUE. Do you smell smoke?

(A beat as they all realize…)

ALL. The enchiladas!!!

(Blackout.)

(A bright, funky disco anthem kicks in – something like "We Are Family [Somos Familia].")*

---

* A license to produce *One of the Good Ones* does not include a performance license for "We Are Family." The publisher and author suggest that the licensee contact ASCAP or BMI to ascertain the music publisher and contact such music publisher to license or acquire permission for performance of the song. If a license or permission is unattainable for "We Are Family," the licensee may not use the song in *One of the Good Ones* but should create an original composition in a similar style or use a similar song in the public domain. For further information, please see the Music and Third-Party Materials Use Note on page iii.